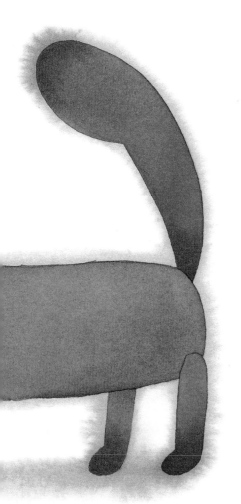

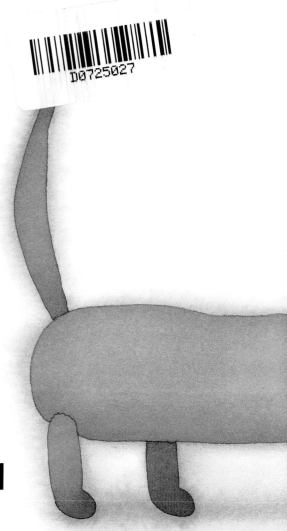

Un gato y un perro

A Cat and a Dog

escrito por **Claire Masurel**

ilustrado por **Bob Kolar**

traducido por Andrés Antreasyan

North South

A Mathilde, C.M.
A Olivia, B.K.

Text copyright © 2001 by Claire Masurel.
Illustrations copyright © 2001 by Bob Kolar.
Spanish translation copyright © 2003 by NorthSouth Books, Inc., New York 10016.

First bilingual edition published in the United States and Canada in 2003 by Ediciones Norte-Sur,
an imprint of NordSüd Verlag AG, CH-8050 Zürich, Switzerland.
Distributed in the United States by NorthSouth Books, Inc., New York 10016.
Spanish text supervised by Sur Editorial Group, Inc.

Library of Congress Cataloging-in-Publicaion Data is available.
Printed in the United States, 2018.
ISBN 978-0-7358-4354-7 (bilingual paperback edition)
1 3 5 7 9 • 10 8 6 4 2

www.northsouth.com

MIX
Paper from
responsible sources
FSC® C003941

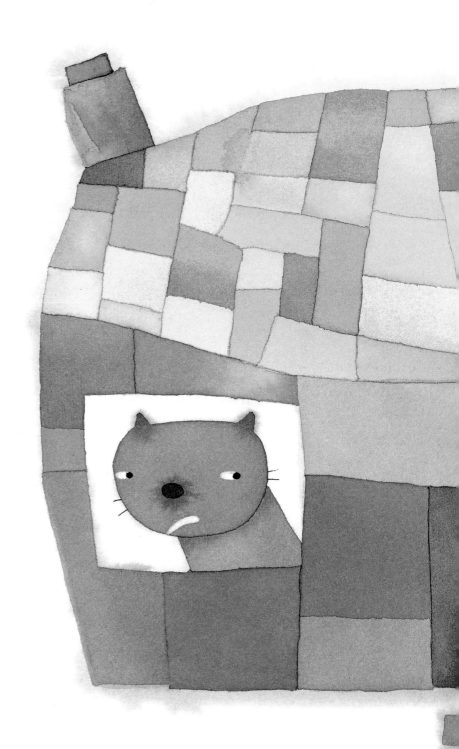

**Un gato y un perro vivían
en la misma casa.**

A cat and a dog lived
in the same house.

Pero no eran amigos.

But they were not friends.

HSSS!

HSSS!

GRRR!

GRRR!

Peleaban todo el tiempo,

They fought all the time,

¡Perro torpe!

Clumsy dog!

noche . . .

night . . .

¡Gato molesto!

Fussy cat!

y día.
and day.

¡Perro sucio!
Dirty dog!

¡Gato perezoso!

Lazy cat!

Peleaban por todo,

They fought about everything,

los mejores lugares,

the best spots,

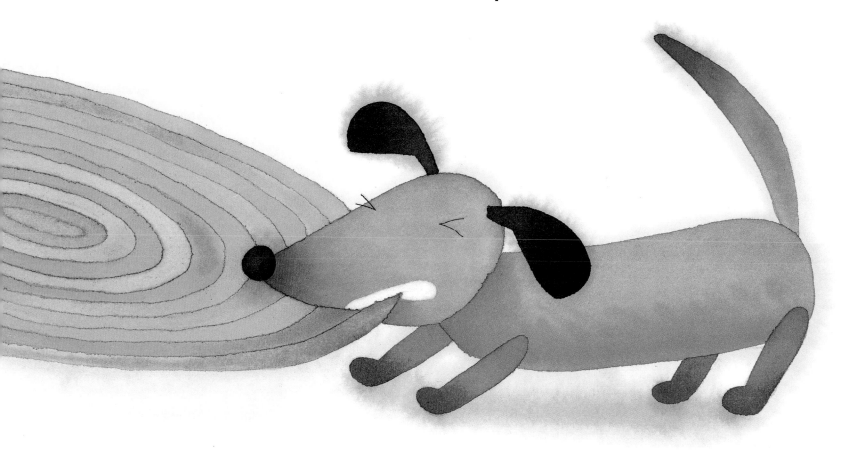

la mejor comida.

the best treats.

Pero más que nada, peleaban por los juguetes.

But most of all, they fought about their toys.

HSSS!

HSSS!

¿Ves estas garras? ¡No te acerques a mi ratoncito!

See these claws? Stay away from my mouse!

GRRR!

GRRR!

¿Ves estos colmillos? ¡No te acerques a mi pelota!
See these fangs? Stay away from my ball!

El gato y el perro jugaban solos.

The cat and the dog played on their own.

Mordisqueando

Chewing

Persiguiendo

Chasing

Rodando

Rolling

Atrapando

Catching

Hasta que un día, pasó algo terrible.

Then one day, something terrible happened.

¡OH, NO!

OH, NO!

No sé nadar.

I can't swim.

¡OH, NO!
OH, NO!

No sé trepar.

I can't climb.

No había absolutamente nada que pudieran hacer.

There was absolutely nothing they could do.

¿Nada?
Nothing?

¡Ya sé!
I know!

¡Ya sé!

I know!

¡Yo sé nadar!

I can swim!

¡Toma, Gato!

Here, Cat!

¡Toma, Perro!

Here, Dog!

**Un gato y un perro viven
en la misma casa . . .**

A cat and a dog live
in the same house . . .

y ahora son los mejores amigos.

and now they are the best of friends.